Portsmouth
CITY COUNCIL
LIBRARY SERVICE   CL-1

D1422666

The diary of
A YOUNG
ROMAN GIRL

Editor Louisa Sladen
Editor-in-Chief John C. Miles
Design Billin Design Solutions
Art Director Jonathan Hair

© 2003 Moira Butterfield

The right of Moira Butterfield to be identified
as the author of this work has been asserted.

First published in 2003
by Franklin Watts
96 Leonard Street
London
EC2A 4XD

Franklin Watts Australia
45-51 Huntley Street
Alexandria
NSW 2015

ISBN 0 7496 4897 X (hbk)
0 7496 5160 1 (pbk)

A CIP catalogue record for this book is available
from the British Library.

Printed in Great Britain

The diary of
A YOUNG
ROMAN GIRL

by Moira Butterfield
Illustrated by Brian Duggan

FRANKLIN WATTS
LONDON•SYDNEY

ALL ABOUT THIS BOOK

This is the fictional diary of Secundia Fulvia
Popillia, a twelve-year-old girl living in ancient
Rome in AD74. Rome was then a bustling city,
capital of an empire stretching as far away
as Britain.

Social rank was important in
Roman times. The most important
person was the **Emperor**.

Next in importance came the
senatorial class, the nobles of Rome.
This included everyone in the Senate
(the Roman parliament).

Next came the **equestrian class**, rich
people who were not members of the
Senate. Popillia's family belong to
this rank.

Next came the **plebeians**, ordinary
Roman citizens.

Below the plebeians were **freedmen**
and **freedwomen**, slaves who had
bought or been given their freedom.

At the bottom were the **slaves**, the
property of their owners.

Roman calendar

The Roman calendar was different from ours.
We have put modern dates in the diary to make
the story clearer. In Roman times, some days had
special names that we have added to the diary:
The first day of the month was the **Kalends**,
The 5th or 7th day (depending on which month)
was called the **Nones**,
The 13th or 15th day (depending on the month)
was called the **Ides**, thought to be an unlucky day.

Roman names

Romans had three names – for instance:
Secundia Fulvia Popillia. 'Secundia' is an official
label, meaning 'second daughter'. 'Fulvia' is the
female version of the family surname 'Fulvius'.
'Popillia' is a personal name, like a modern first
name.

Roman marriage

In this diary we have used facts that we know
about Roman life to try to imagine what life
would have been like for Popillia. We know that
by law Roman girls could marry at the age of
twelve, and boys at fourteen, but this didn't
mean they had to, and they often waited until
they were a little older.

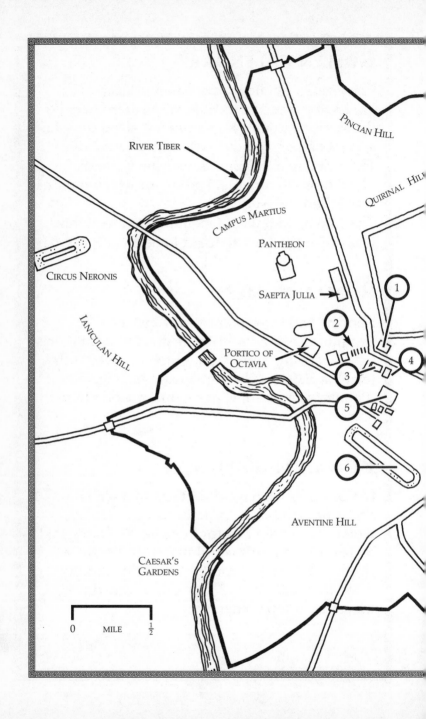

ANCIENT ROME
AD74

CASTRA PRAETORIA

VIMINAL HILL

ESQUILINE HILL

CAELIAN HILL

7

1 CURIA (SENATE HOUSE)
2 GEMONIAN STAIRS
3 FORUM ROMANUM,
  THE MAIN CITY SQUARE,
  SURROUNDED BY
  IMPORTANT TEMPLES
4 TEMPLE OF VESTA
5 EMPEROR'S PALACE
6 CIRCUS MAXIMUS
  (FOR CHARIOT RACING)
7 VIA APPIA – THE MAIN
  ROAD TO THE SOUTH
  OF ROME

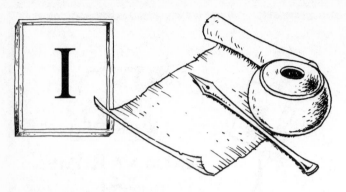

14 April AD74
Popillia's house, outside Rome

"Popi! Popi! Popi! I've found a frog in the
fountain!"

Aren't six-year-olds noisy? You notice that
when you're nearly thirteen. Having Dio as a
little brother has its uses, though. For one thing
he's still got Paetas. Greek slaves make the best
tutors, so Father says, but Paetas has his hands
full with Dio, who prefers to gallop around the
corridors of our villa pretending to be a
horseman than learn stuffy old letters and
numbers. I think Paetas is quite pleased that I
sneak into their lessons.

I'll never forget when my dear old tutor
Cosmus retired. I was only seven, and I cried
for days. I know Cosmus had taught the
family's children for years, and it was
wonderful that Father gave him his freedom,
but for me it was a big blow, as it seemed to be
the end of my education.

Father tried to explain: "Popillia, you know
your letters and your numbers, so what's the

problem? To marry well it's more import
you to start brushing up your home skill
is your weaving, for instance?"

That didn't help me feel better, but before
Cosmus left he told me: "Popillia, you have a
bright mind. Don't forget it, and though you are
a woman, try to use it when you can."

So, with the help of Paetas, I try not to forget.
Mother knows I sit in with Dio at lesson times
and she doesn't mind. I think she's told Father
not to worry about me being there because she
understands that I really want to carry on. She's
busy herself most days anyway, visiting friends
or running the household.

Paetas says I write well but if I want to improve
I should practise every day.

"Write what you know," he says.

So today I've found a quiet shady corner of
the garden where I can write and hear the birds
singing at the same time. I didn't think I'd be
disturbed. But little chance of that! Dio has
already charged by twice waving a wooden
sword. Our household slave, Paulina, has been
shuffling past too, peering over my shoulder
while she was pretending to sweep.

There's no sign of Mother, or my stepsister,
Cecilia. They went out in the family litter first
thing, to ransack the shops. Since Cecilia has
agreed to a marriage with Melus there's been a
shopping frenzy for the wedding. Cecilia is on

9

a mission to see and compare every flame-coloured bridal veil in Rome. Paulina says that's what happens when you're fifteen. Your head fills up with shopping lists. I'm glad Cecilia is so happy to be married, though. I can't imagine it happening to me, not yet anyway. I certainly couldn't be bothered with all that shopping.

Father's out on business. I'm guessing that my big stepbrother Longus will be spending his day cheering at the chariot racing.

And me? So much for peace and quiet. Here comes Dio again with something cupped in his hand. "I've caught a frog, Popi! Do you want to touch it?"

15 APRIL AD74

It's all very well for Paetas to say: "Write what you know", but, as I told him, I live in a deadly quiet part of Rome and spend most of my time in our villa, so my life isn't exactly full of battles and adventures. I don't want to waste ink just writing about the daily comings and goings of the Flavius family: *Got up. Had honey cake for breakfast. Wore tunic as usual.*

When I mentioned this to Paetas he laughed and said: "I think you'll be surprised how interesting the Flavius family will seem, once you think about it." Hmm. Maybe.

He suggested I could make my diary more interesting by writing down festival dates and official religious ceremonies, which will take up space, since there's one nearly every day in Rome. Some of them go back hundreds of years to when Rome was a small town. That's why we sometimes have weird traditions even Paetas doesn't fully understand. But he says I should: "Write about them as if you are explaining them to someone who lives far away on the edge of the Roman Empire."

So here goes:

Today is part of the ten-day Festival of Ceres, goddess of farming. This particular day is called Fordicidia, when eight cows will be sacrificed in honour of Tellus, the earth goddess.

Well, sorry, Paetas, it sounds one long yawn to me, though I know exactly what Father would say: "These ceremonies are vital to the good of Rome, Popillia."

I know, I know. It's just that some of them are, well, dull.

Paetas has just taken a look at my first writing effort. He said that it was mostly fine but I didn't try very hard with the Fordicidia festival. So let's take a look at the Flavius family instead, and see if I can make us as interesting as Paetas says we are.

We're from a long line of spice importers and I guess you could call us rich. We're of equestrian rank – not top nobility, but we're well able to pay our way. We have a spacious house with smart wall paintings and plenty of slaves, but what Father would dearly like is for a bit more 'breeding', a hike up the social ladder. That means going up a notch to senatorial rank, which is where we children come in.

In a perfect world his oldest son, my stepbrother Longus, would do the business, getting himself elected to important government offices and forging an unstoppable path up the senatorial career ladder. Only Longus isn't co-operating as yet, and besides, it's a drop of that old established Roman noble blood that Father is after for the family status.

'Marry up,' is his solution, and my stepsister Cecilia has done him proud by catching the eye of Vibius Decius Melus, shining son of a noble senator, no less. Actually Melus is all right and when he visits he usually brings little presents for me and Dio – a pot of honey or a bottle of orange water.

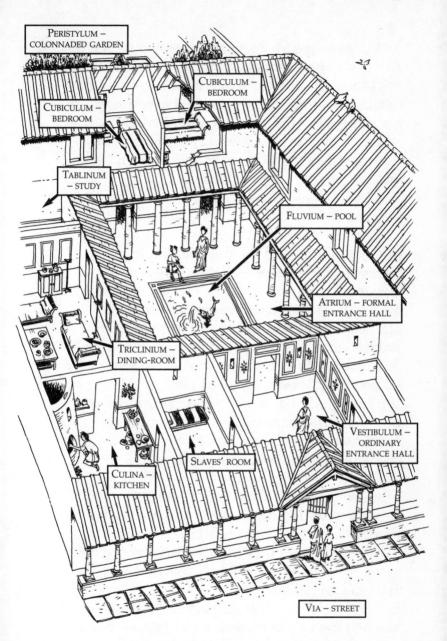

PERISTYLUM – COLONNADED GARDEN

CUBICULUM – BEDROOM

CUBICULUM – BEDROOM

TABLINUM – STUDY

FLUVIUM – POOL

CUBICULUM – BEDROOM

ATRIUM – FORMAL ENTRANCE HALL

TRICLINIUM – DINING-ROOM

VESTIBULUM – ORDINARY ENTRANCE HALL

SLAVES' ROOM

CULINA – KITCHEN

VIA – STREET

VILLA OF THE FULVIUS FAMILY, WHERE POPILLIA LIVES

13

Longus says Melus's family may put on airs and graces but they need our money and Melus might not be so friendly if Father wasn't giving Cecilia a whopping big slice of it as a dowry on her marriage. This just isn't true. Longus is turning into a cynic. Does it come with being seventeen? Where is he anyway? I haven't seen him in days, not even at dinner.

I asked Atia, our old slave, if she knew where Longus was.

"No, sweetpea," Atia replied. "Nicander says he's out all hours of the day and night."

"Atia, don't gossip!" Nicander snapped, interrupting us and doing his stuffy, head-slave act. I suppose it's not surprising that he's a bit old-fashioned because Father has owned him since he was a kid and Father is just the same.

Then Dio found us and started chanting what I'd just said: "Have you seen Longus? Have you seen Longus?" he sang out, skipping around eagerly. It was harmless enough until Father came round the corner looking thunderous, with beads of sweat all over his forehead.

"Have you seen Longus?" Dio trilled again.

"Gods, you make the roof tiles rattle with your confounded noise, boy! Straighten your tunic!" he barked. Then he glared at me.

"And you, Popillia, your hair is a bird's nest! In a year or two you will be a married woman. Start looking like one!"

That comment showed that Father was really in a bad mood. He knew it would upset me.

Later on he came to look for Dio and me and gave us a shamefaced smile. He patted Dio's head and gave me a flower he had picked from the garden.

Poor old Father. He's very worried but I'm not sure why.

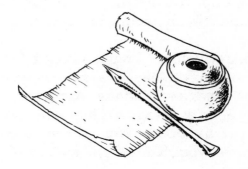

20 April ad74

"Popi, wake up. You're to have your hair done!"
Cecilia burst into my room and announced this
morning.

"Paulina will do it," I replied sleepily.

"No, not today! Melus's mother has sent us
one of her slaves as a kindness. Apparently
she's very good at doing wedding styles and
wants to practise on me. While she's at it she's
going to dress your hair too and make you look
all grown up."

I am not happy about this, so I am being extra
slow getting ready. I have decided to sit in my
room and write in my diary until they come and
drag me out. It means I'm going to miss Paetas's
lesson this morning, and instead I'm going to
have my hair pulled about, pinned and smeared
with goo, until I look like an idiot. I don't want
to be grown up, not yet.

Well, it wasn't quite as bad as I thought. The hairdresser appeared with two assistants and baskets full of equipment.

"Who is the bride?" she asked grandly, in a bossy voice that made me giggle. She sat Cecilia in a wicker chair and put her hand out with a flourish. One of her assistants handed her a bent iron spearhead and she began to part Cecilia's hair with it for the wedding style.

"Oh, that's uncomfortable!" Cecilia began. The hairdresser's eyebrows shot up as if she'd been called a rude name.

"I assure you, this is the traditional tool used on the hair of brides. Nothing else would possibly do," she replied firmly. Cecilia shut up. The woman carried on, prattling on to Mother about the grand weddings she'd been involved with. "I did the oldest Auralius girl, of course. What a wonderful wedding! She had special almonds brought all the way from Egypt…"

But, self-important as she was, she did a great job on Cecilia's hair. It looked wonderful.

"There, you look lovely. This is exactly what we'll do on the day," she finished. Then she glanced sideways at Mother. "Tell me, will the family's oldest son be wanting his hair cut before the wedding?" she asked, raising her eyebrows slightly at the mention of my stepbrother.

"No, no," Mother replied shortly.

"Very well…" she murmured, and went quiet, although it was obvious she had got something else to say. Instead she turned to me and eyed my mass of unruly curls. Then she began to hunt through her baskets for a stronger comb.

21 APRIL AD74

We all had dinner together today to celebrate Rome being founded by Romulus. Our cook Atia made the special millet cakes and fresh milk heated with wine.

Big brother Longus arrived home for dinner and I almost wish he hadn't. He and Father sniped at each other the whole time.

"So you remember where you live, then? I was beginning to wonder," Father started.

There was silence and a sullen look from Longus. "Is your toga decent for the wedding?" Father tried again. "Or is it stained with wine and candle grease from your drunken nights on the town?" he snapped.

Longus stood up abruptly, slammed down his wine cup and strode off without another word.

"Be here tomorrow for lunch! I want to talk to you!" Father called after him angrily. Mother fiddled with her brooch pin, something she only does when she's worried. I guessed she would have liked to say something. Knowing her, she'd like to tell Father to go easy on Longus.

But Father doesn't like being told how to handle him. Instead Mother turned to me: "You will go to Cornelia's tomorrow, Popillia. And Dio, I have asked Paetas to take you to see the sacred geese."

"But I've seen them loads of times!" complained Dio, realising, like me, that we were being sent out of the way.

"Well, check they're still safe and sound," Mother replied lamely.

"Of course they are! If they die, Rome gets destroyed! Everybody knows that!" Dio answered back indignantly.

"Just go!" Mother insisted and shoved a piece of flatbread into his mouth to shut him up.

Now I'm in my room but I can hear that Mother and Father are still talking in the garden. It sounds like she's trying to calm him down.

22 APRIL AD74

Slaves have whisked me off in the family litter to Cornelia's villa next door. She is nine years old and obsessed with being a Vestal Virgin at the moment. I remember I used to enjoy playing at being a priestess, too, but nowadays I'm beginning to get bored by Cornelia's games. I'm too old to be chosen as a Vestal Virgin now, anyway, because you have to be between seven and ten when you start the job. The Temple of Vesta didn't need a new trainee when I was the right age. If you get chosen you have to go and live in the Vestal Virgins' house with all the other priestesses, and spend the next thirty years tending the sacred flame in the Temple.

"You get consulted by important people!" Cornelia tells me. "And you get lots of privileges, and it's a really important job keeping the goddess happy."

That's all true, but if you ever broke the rules – got married or had a lover – you'd get buried alive. No question. That's the law.

Anyway, Cornelia likes the idea but Longus says she has no chance because the choosing is fixed so the daughter of some top family always gets any vacant position. Cornelia's father isn't that important, so I think she'll be disappointed.

This morning, Cornelia's mother Julia came gliding in to see us. She was looking very elegant, as always, in a blue silk tunic and expensive-looking gold earrings. She sometimes lets us try on her jewellery and even use her make-up, drawing round our eyes with smudgy black so they look twice as big and dreamy, and dabbing cinnamon-scented perfume on us from a little flask.

Anyway, today she was more mysterious than usual. She said something really strange: "I do

21

hope your mother is bearing up. Problems take their toll," she murmured.

"Oh, you mean the wedding preparations?" I replied. "I think it's all going to plan. The engagement ceremony will be soon."

"I do hope so…" she said, as if there was some doubt. To my amazement, I thought she looked sorry for me.

"What was your mother on about?" I asked Cornelia later. "No idea," she replied. "Come on. Let's pretend we're carrying sacred water pots on our heads."

I have begun to feel worried. Has Melus done something to ruin the wedding? Or, worse still, has Cecilia disgraced herself – kissed a bathhouse attendant or something? I'd be amazed if either of them had done anything to jeopardise being together; I've never seen a couple look so happy together.

When I got home later I found Atia repairing Longus's toga. It certainly looked a bit battered.

"Atia, is everything all right about the wedding?" I asked, thinking the slaves would be bound to know what was what.

"Hold this corner," she said, laying the toga out flat.

"So, is there a problem?" I persisted. Atia has been with the family a long time. She was here in this house the day Father's first wife Claudia died, the day Cecilia was born. She knows us all inside-out, and I could tell straight away she knew something now.

"Longus and your father aren't getting along, I know that. He didn't come home for lunch today although your father asked him to," Atia explained. "But I'm sure it will sort itself out. Are you looking forward to the wedding?"

"Yes, I suppose I am," I replied. "Cecilia and Melus are going to be really happy together, aren't they?" Atia smiled and stroked my hair, just like she always did when I was small.

"It'll be your turn soon enough. You'll marry and give away all your toys, and go to live with your husband's family. It seems only yesterday that you were tiny!" That made me feel sad.

"I don't want to leave home," I murmured.

"But you don't want to play baby games either, do you," Atia replied. "Just now you're in-between."

"I suppose," I replied.

Atia dug her hand into her tunic and gave me a handful of sweet nuts to munch, and I forgot what I was going to ask. Come to think of it, that was very clever of Atia.

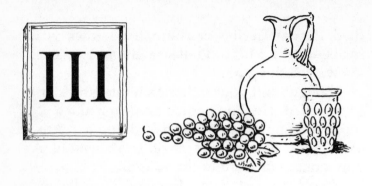

III

23 APRIL AD74

"Popi, it's Vinalia Day. Paetas said so," Dio announced first thing this morning. "A priest is going to kill a lamb for Jupiter and pick the new grapes, and lots of people are going to drink so much wine that they fall over."

Dio can be annoyingly clever for a six-year-old. What he didn't predict, though, was a big new Vinalia event in our house – a flaming row.

I nearly missed it. After lunch I was packed off to Cornelia's house again but I came home in time for dinner and my litter arrived at the front door at the same time as Melus. I could tell he had just come from a bathhouse because his face was smooth-looking and he smelt strongly of sandalwood, Cecilia's favourite scent.

"Hello, Popi. Have you been out partying for Vinalia?" he joked.

"No such luck," I replied. Then Nicander opened the front door to us both, and his eyes

almost popped out with panic when he saw
Melus alongside me. As we stepped inside we
heard raised voices.

"You dare to come here and tell me what to
do. Tell *me*!" Father was barking. "You will
disgrace us, that's what you'll do!"

"I'm sick of this!" Longus was shouting back.

"I? I? Gods, stop thinking of yourself for
once! Think of your sisters – the wedding!"
Father raged.

Nicander looked terrified and half ran ahead
of us through the entrance hall, forgetting to help
Melus take off his cloak.

"I don't have to accept this! I'm going and I'm not coming back!" Longus cried, and burst out of the dining-room. He stormed past us as if we were invisible and strode out into the street through the open front door.

"That boy may be seventeen, but I'd whip him if I could!" Father was still shouting. "By Hades, in the old times I could have killed him and not been punished!"

"Lucius!" Mother gasped.

"All right, all right! Of course I didn't mean that," Father blustered. In the background we could hear the sound of Cecilia's sobbing.

Nicander rushed ahead of us into the dining-room and gabbled to Father that Melus was paying a visit. Then he actually seemed to put his arm out to prevent us from going in, but he couldn't do that without pushing Melus, so his arm dropped limply as Melus stepped past him, and Nicander let him through.

Then I slipped through the doorway behind Melus, unnoticed. Father froze and stared at the visitor, horrified. Mother gasped, and Cecilia jumped up with her hands to her face.

"Oh, Melus!" she sobbed and ran out.

Poor old Melus stood there, utterly confused, and so did I.

Then Father managed to recover himself and he got up from his couch and stepped forward to greet Melus with a false smile that looked far too wide.

"Melus, my dear boy. Come in, come in. Share some Vinalia wine with us in honour of Venus. I'm sorry about that little incident. Just a harmless disagreement over expenses. Longus gets through his allowance quicker than water runs through sand."

"But Cecilia… Is she well?" Melus asked anxiously.

"Oh yes. Nerves about the wedding, no doubt; perhaps not enough water in her wine tonight… She's a very steady girl normally. Please, sit on a couch. Have some Vinalia wine, Melus," Father blustered.

"Popillia, dear. Run along to your room," Mother muttered to me, and I did, but not before I heard Melus making a Vinalia toast.

"In honour of Venus, goddess of beauty and love." I glanced at Father. His smile was oddly frozen on his face.

It's getting dark and I shall have to get an oil lamp lit in my room if I want to keep writing. I've just heard Melus say goodbye and go on his way, and now it's quiet in our house. Out in Rome I expect it's quite noisy, what with the Vinalia drinking games that go on. I don't know much about them, but I'll bet Longus does. I hope he's all right.

24 APRIL AD74

Father was like thunder at breakfast, and Mother was really touchy, which isn't at all like her. She said I couldn't go to Cornelia's house, as planned.

When I asked why she snapped: "Don't answer back, child." She hasn't made her usual visit to friends this morning, either.

When I saw Paetas I asked him what was going on, but he made me nearly explode with irritation by saying: "I don't gossip. Anyway, as a writer you should explore other people's actions for yourself."

Paetas, that was so pompous! (And I don't care if you read this one day.)

Cecilia hasn't appeared yet. It's time to put my papyrus away, knock on her door and find out what's really been happening.

There's certainly a lot more going on in this house than I realised. I found Cecilia moping in her room. Her cheeks were blotchy from crying and she was pointlessly pulling the threads out of the fringe of a cushion.

"It's Longus. He's ruined everything!" she burst out. "He's completely selfish! I hate him!"

"Why? Where is he?" I asked.

"He's gone and he says he's not coming back. Oh, Popi! It's not fair! Melus won't be allowed to marry me, and I love him so!" We hugged each other. Then she told me everything.

"Longus says he's going to marry without Father's permission, and worse still, he wants to marry a freedwoman, an ex-slave! She's from… from… northern Africa, somewhere miles away." Her eyes widened and she leant forward to tell me her biggest news: "She's a rope-dancer!"

I think something intelligent like, "Oh…" came out of my mouth. I was amazed, but still a bit confused.

"A dancer? What, you mean the sort people hire to dance at parties and dinners?" I asked.

"Worse! This one performs at a theatre! Anyone can watch her! She dances in the intervals with a rope, and pretends it's a snake. Once Melus's family find out about her they'll call the wedding off. They won't want anything to do with us!" Writer or not, this time I was really lost for words. Now they're betrothed, I can't imagine Cecilia without Melus. It's a real calamity.

IV

1 MAY AD74
THE KALENDS OF MAY

They've decorated the city with flowers because it's the festival of Floralia. I know because I saw them and they were especially pretty around the Temple of Flora. Yes, I *was* allowed out, but only if I stayed in the litter. It was such a relief after being cooped up indoors for days.

"Keep out of the public gaze," Father had said. "I don't want anyone asking awkward questions. We must keep the lid on the gossip for a little while, until I find the boy and talk to him. I've told people you all have colds."

This lie worked on poor Melus, who hasn't visited since Vinalia but has been sending Cecilia daily gifts of honeycombs, fruit and big baskets full of mint to cure colds.

Atia says that Longus has gone well and truly missing, and apparently the rope-dancer is out of town. They could even have got married by now. What a mess. I don't care about myself getting married to anyone, but I do care about Cecilia and Melus being together and I care very much about Longus, too. The trouble is that he and Father only communicate by shouting.

Someone needs to find Longus and really *talk* to him. That's why I did what I did today.

I begged to see the Floralia flower displays, as if my life depended on it, and eventually Father agreed as long as I didn't talk to anyone. Then Dio wanted to come with me, but I got into the litter and hurried the slaves on before he could get Father's permission.

Once I was away from the house I insisted that the poor young slaves who were carrying me take me to all the places that Longus normally went. I'm not at all bullying like that normally, though I know some who are, but it was the only way to get what I wanted. I was sure they could show me places Father hadn't thought of looking.

Nicander will be very angry with the slaves when he hears where they took me, but I'll explain I threatened them with punishment unless they obeyed me, and he can be angry with me instead. I didn't feel good about doing it, but one of us has to find Longus!

First of all, the slaves carried me to the bathhouse where Longus goes every day to get bathed and shaved. Of course, I couldn't go in to a men-only place like that, but there was a door attendant who looked very surprised when

I popped my head out from behind the litter's curtains. I asked if he knew my brother.

"Yes, Madam. Normally he comes here every afternoon... He takes exercise and bathes."

"Have you seen him in the last few days?" I asked, and he replied that he hadn't. He seemed honest enough and refused payment for his answers, so I suppose I should believe him.

Then we went to a noisier more crowded street lined with shops and stalls piled high with goods that spilled out on to the side of the road. We stopped at a small food and drink shop. Longus sometimes sits on a stool here, apparently, watching the world go by. It wasn't very clean. There were pools of wine slopped on to the marble counter, along with some bar snacks for sale – a pot of half-eaten stew and some bowls of lentil mush. There was even one customer fast asleep in a corner. Father would have a fit if he knew I'd stood there talking to the barman. The barman took some coins but denied knowing Longus, though I've heard that barmen generally keep their customers' secrets.

I got back in the litter and sat there miserably. What would a young man do if he argued with his family? Where would he go? I was so desperate I ordered the slaves to take me all the way to the stables of the Blues, because I knew they were Longus's favourite chariot-racing team. This would really be going a step too far for Father, I knew, because the sort of women who turn up outside the stables are adoring fans crazy to meet the drivers, and I was really risking my reputation as a nicely brought-up lady if anyone recognised me.

There were a couple of men lounging under an archway. They looked me up and down quite openly and I could feel my cheeks go pink. "I'm looking for my brother, Lucius Fulvius Longus," I explained.

"Longus… I know him," said one of the men. "He bets at the chariot track. Comes here for racing tips, sometimes. So you've lost him, then?" he grinned, highly amused. "Oh dear, oh dear. That's bad news, that is. Has he run away from home, the naughty boy? I'll tell you what. There's a gladiator-training school around the corner. Perhaps he's signed on there!" He laughed loudly at the idea.

"Longus? He's no gladiator," the second man grunted. His arms were muscly and he looked tough. He must have seen the tears in my eyes, as he spoke to me a little more kindly.

"Go home, girl. This is no place for you. You should be at home with your mother. Look, I'll keep an ear to the ground for news of your brother. Where do you live? All right then, off you go. And don't fret about him. I've seen him training at the bathhouse. He can look after himself."

It was later than I thought when I got home, and I went quickly to my room, complaining of a headache. I'm still hiding in here, because I've a strong feeling I'm about to find myself in big trouble.

2 MAY AD74

Nicander found out what I did and told Father. Traitor. Father called me to his study. His lips were narrow and bloodless with anger. It looked as if he wanted to explode with fury, but he was keeping it in – for the moment.

"You will go to the farm, along with your brother and stepsister. Tell Paulina to pack your things at once," he said sharply.

"But I… " I began.

That was it, as if I'd cracked him like a water pipe. Words came pouring out of him.

"No! You will not question me or be disobedient again! You toured the streets of Rome in the family litter, as plain as you like! For Jupiter's sake; it's got the family initials on it! Did you think nobody would notice? Gods! It's bad enough having a son who flouts my authority and condemns the family to disgrace. Now my daughter is intent on making it worse!"

"I just wanted to find him, for Cecilia's sake," I sobbed. At that he sat down. His shoulders slumped and the anger seemed to drain out of him.

"I know, I know, Popi. But it's probably too late. Melus's family have not yet agreed to a date for the official engagement ceremony, let alone the wedding. I think they're delaying it deliberately. They may have smelt scandal. Your mother says that hairdressing slave they sent was trying to find something out. If there is disgrace they'll want to keep their son out of it. Until the engagement he has no obligations to us."

A silence fell over us both then.

Finally, Father stood up and touched my arm. He is quick-tempered, but he can never be angry for long.

"It'll be calmer and quieter for you at the farm. Try to give Cecilia some comfort, and keep

Dio from telling our troubles to everyone he meets, all right? Paetas told me you're doing some writing. You could take it with you and keep yourself busy, eh?"

"Father, is it so bad if Longus marries a freedwoman?" I asked. "Yes, Popillia. And worse still, she's nothing but a rope-dancer. God knows, I've given up on the boy ever doing what I ask of him, and if we can't get noble blood in the family, well, I suppose we shall survive. But this is bad for Cecilia," he sighed heavily. "She's in love; anyone can see, but Melus's father is from one of the grandest families in Rome. He won't touch us with a boat pole if he gets wind of a scandal like this... and when you come to marry, it could count against *you*, too. A rope-dancer!" Father hit the table with his fist in frustration.

There was nothing more to say, so I left him pacing up and down.

9 May ad74

Now I'm at the farm, I feel as if I'm six years old again. I'm taken back by the smell of the meadow grass that was once higher than my head, the bleating of the goats I once thought were so big and the way the light comes through the villa windows and scatters across tiny details on the wall paintings I know so well – the basket of fruit, the peacock and the bee in the flower.

Since I came last year there are some new black and white mosaics through one of the corridors and new heating in the bathhouse, but apart from that it is just the same.

The journey from Rome was bumpy, as usual, but I like it when the city peters out into the countryside. Then I know it's not all that far to the farm. We made quite a procession, with two covered carts and some slaves. Mother put her foot down with Father and insisted on staying in Rome in case there was news of Longus, but Paetas has come with us to make sure Dio keeps up with his studies (and to keep a close eye on us, on Father's orders). He's suggested that I could try writing some poetry while I'm away. I might.

"Here come the little ones!" old Gallio cried, hobbling out to greet us when we rattled up the hill and finally arrived in the farm courtyard. Other slaves have come and gone, but Gallio has stayed here, along with Verina, for years and years, running the estate for Father's family.

I think he has got a little more stooped since I saw him last year, though.

"Not so little!" he chuckled when I and Cecilia climbed down from the cart, followed by Dio.

Verina rushed out from the villa and fussed over us. "There you are, my dears! You look pale, Cecilia. I have honey and bread and fresh goat's milk laid out on the table under the trees. Come on now, eat. Dio, you look more like your father every day."

The bread was nutty, rough and fresh, and while we licked the honey off our fingers the bees that made it worked behind us, humming in the olive groves.

Cecilia and I used the little bathhouse to soak the dust of the road away. I thought this might be a good time to try and cheer Cecilia up a little so I told her what I had been thinking on our journey from Rome.

"I know Longus won't let us down, Cecilia. Not when it really matters. This row... I think in some way it might be about him and Father, and it's stopped him thinking clearly. But I don't think he will stay away."

Cecilia looked up hopefully through her long black eyelashes, and for a moment she looked just like Longus. I'm sure he will think of her before he does anything really crazy. After their mother Claudia died, Longus always wanted to help look after his baby sister, even though he must have been only toddling himself. Atia told me.

14 MAY AD74

There was a vivid sunset today and I sat outside watching it with Gallio as Dio capered round, holding Cecilia's hand, dancing in and out of the grape-press building, and making her laugh.

Nowadays Gallio has stiff limbs. "I move less but I order others around more," he says. Today he had one of his stories to tell me. He knows I love to hear them.

"The Greeks worshipped Apollo on this day, in the old times," he murmured. "Apollo was born this day on the island of Delos, and they say that on his birth the island was covered with golden flowers and encircled by swans."

Not for the first time I wondered how much Gallio could remember about his childhood in Greece, before he was bought by Grandfather at a slave market. I don't know if he was kidnapped or taken in some kind of battle or sold by his family, like Paetas was.

"Have you ever seen Delos?" I asked.

"No, Popillia," he replied and left it at that.

We sat watching the redness of the clouds turn to orange and purple, and then, because I trust him, I told him about Cecilia and Melus, and how Longus had left home.

He nodded his head and said nothing, but then Verina came out with a flask of sweet honey mead and some tiny blue glasses. She sat with us and had plenty to say when I retold the news.

"Why all the fuss? He could keep this rope-dancer as a mistress. It's quite common. I hear the Emperor Vespasian himself has a mistress, a freedwoman as well. But I suppose that might not do for Melus's family if they think a lot of themselves. Typical hypocritical Roman snobs by the sound of it."

Gallio raised his eyebrows but obviously knew it was useless trying to stop Verina in full flow.

She started again. "I can see that marriage wouldn't do. With a freedwoman as a wife Longus could wave goodbye to moving up the social ladder. He should keep her as a secret mistress. That'd be the answer."

MAIN HOUSE

PIGEON LOFT

WELL

GEESE AND CHICKENS

42

THE FULVIUS FARM

OLIVE TREES

OLIVE PRESS

BEEHIVES

WHEAT

43

Gallio stood up stiffly and slowly, and Verina immediately stood to help him. Together they looked like any old married couple, except, of course they are slaves – so they can't marry in law. I don't think they ever had children together. If there were any, Father would own them, and they'd be working for us here or in Rome, so I'd know about it.

I suppose we are their family, now. I know Verina was in the room when Father's first wife Claudia died in childbirth.

I often think about Claudia these days, wondering what she was like. Claudia died when she was only a year older than Cecilia is now. Did she look like her children? Does Father ever think of her?

It's not unusual to die in childbirth; I know that. I wish I didn't. It's a scary thought, because it seems whether I like it or not, I'll have to get married and have children myself, some day. I'm not sure I like that idea at all.

15 MAY AD74
THE IDES OF MAY

Dio came in and sprinkled water on my head
this morning, making some blotches on my
papyrus as I wrote.

"Grant us the favour of Mercury, god of
merchants!" he chanted and then rushed off
outside to sprinkle the farm geese. It's the
Festival of Mercury and Paetas must have
reminded him. Father will sprinkle sacred water
around his warehouse for good business luck,
but I don't think the water Dio used was sacred.
I think he got it from the well bucket.

Now Dio is shouting out that he can see
someone riding up the hill towards the farm. He
says it looks like Melus!

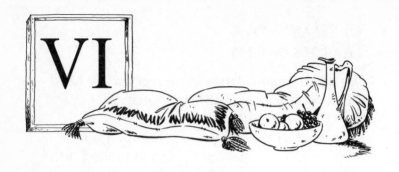

VI

16 MAY AD74

Yesterday was the best day in ages. It turns out
that Melus just couldn't stay away from Cecilia
any longer. Her delight was plain when she saw
him. "Sometimes marriage comes first, and love
grows in time," I remember Mother telling me (I
never dared ask, but I guessed that had
happened to her). Cecilia has found both at
once, I hope.

Melus joined us for a snack of cheese and
olives. Cecilia held on to his arm all the while
as if he might disappear again. He smiled, but
his eyes looked worried and then he spoke to
us openly.

"I've searched for Longus but without
success, and I know your parents have found no
clues to his whereabouts either. The worst thing
is that now my parents know something's up.
There's always some nosy neighbour or
talkative slave to spread bad news. Luckily

word hasn't gone round about any dancing girl, yet. Yes, I made your father tell me everything, but I've kept it quiet. My parents only know the general story – Longus has gone off in a huff after a row with your father about his general behaviour – fairly typical family stuff."

Melus nervously pushed an olive around his plate as he spoke. "My mother and father aren't happy. They suspect there's something more, but I've persuaded them to hold off from confronting your father, and to give him some time. They've agreed for my sake, but my father won't allow an engagement ceremony to go ahead. He advised me not to see you in case a scandal broke and—"

At that, Cecilia dissolved in tears. Melus looked desperate.

"No, no, Cecilia. It will be all right! Don't cry! Popillia, don't you have the slightest notion where Longus might have gone?"

We racked our brains and went over Longus's favourite haunts again, but Melus had already searched them all.

"I feel so powerless out here on the farm!" Cecilia groaned.

"I know, my love. But your father is only doing what he thinks best, to keep you away from rumours," Melus assured her.

"Does Father know you're here?" I asked.

"Yes. Your mother told him it would be cruel to prevent a visit."

"And your parents?" Cecilia added.

"Ah, well. As I said, they advised me to avoid contact for the moment, but I could as soon do that as stop breathing! I told them I would go away for a few days to my cousin's estate. It's within riding distance, luckily."

This was news to me. "It's my cousin Livia. You'll like her!" grinned Melus.

18 MAY AD74

Cecilia has gone to meet Livia, the mysterious cousin who is visiting from Rome to check on her farms. Apparently she wasn't planning to, but Melus persuaded her to come, to give him an excuse to see Cecilia. I wasn't invited on the trip, which made me really cross.

"Dio needs one of us to stay here," Cecilia explained, cuddling up to Melus.

"What about you? You should have a chaperone!" I whined grumpily.

"I'm taking Paetas!" she snapped back, then asked me not to tell Mother she had gone without me. This family is going out of control!

20 MAY AD74

Cecilia has come back bursting with praise for Livia. "She is so funny. You must see her hair. She has lovely clothes," and so on, and so on. Apparently I will get my chance to meet her soon because she's invited us all over in three days' time.

Cecilia and I were sitting outside when Dio came up behind us and made us jump. We chased him around the garden, giggling, just as if we were all little children together. I wish Longus had been there, too, and it could have been just like it used to be before he and Father began to row so much.

After dinner we heard more from Cecilia about the amazing Livia.

"She's divorced. She had an arranged marriage to some old man when she was still very young, and they fought like a cat and a dog in a bag. Eventually they just couldn't bear each other any more and he agreed to divorce her. She went back to her father's house, minus a slice of the wedding dowry. Then her father died and being an only child she got all the property and money, and now she can please herself. Wait until you meet her, Popi!"

24 MAY AD74

We travelled over to Livia's grand villa yesterday. It had any number of marble colonnades, the finest mosaics, costly hangings and a cushion-filled room with open sides that looks out over a slope and a river. Livia herself was wearing expensive green clothes that showed off her red hair. Melus told us she was twenty-two but her face looked younger. She was very friendly, and as soon as she spoke to me she made me feel important.

"I've heard all about you, Popillia. Your sister says you are a keen writer. I must show you the library later."

Since yesterday was Tubilustrium, Vulcan's day, Livia laid on a little show for us, with local dancers and a man dressed up as Vulcan, blacksmith of the gods. His face was all sooty, as if he'd been busy working all day in his forge. Musicians played flutes and little shiny trumpets to imitate the divine trumpets that Vulcan made for the gods. It was great fun.

Later on it was obvious that Melus and Cecilia were going to spend the rest of the evening staring into each other's eyes, so Livia steered me away to the library as promised, where there was roll after roll of poetry, philosophy and history – scrolls her father had collected. I could have spent hours there but it was getting dark, so instead we sat in a courtyard with lamps suspended around it. Soon we started talking, as if we were old friends.

"Will you marry soon, Popillia?" Livia asked, giving me a mischievous look.

"Not yet," I replied, startled by the question. Then I decided to be mischievous back.

"You are… divorced?" I ventured. Then I felt embarrassed at what I'd said, but it turned out Livia didn't mind me asking.

"Yes, and it's a relief, I can tell you. My

husband and I weren't like those two in the
dining-room. I agreed to the match because
I was young and my father wanted it, but love
didn't develop and after a while my husband
and I stayed at opposite ends of the house,
believe me!"

"You weren't sorry to part, then?" I asked.

"No, it was the best thing, and we had no
children, so it was easier. Lots of people divorce
these days, after all. Now I have some freedom
and luckily I have the money to go with it."

"Will you marry again soon?" I ventured.

"We'll see," she smiled. "And what about
you, Popi? What are your dreams for the future?"

I felt so comfortable with Livia, she seemed so straightforward and honest, that I told her something I've never said to anyone before, or even really thought through properly in my own head.

"Livia, I don't ever want to get married. I don't want anything to change. I don't want to be grown-up and I don't want to have to leave home, and… and…"

Livia looked at me expectantly, and because I trusted her, and because I suppose it was time I said it to someone, I admitted a secret I'd been hiding even from myself. "Cecilia's mother, Claudia, died in childbirth when she was really young. Nobody talks about it at home. I don't like to ask my mother about it. What if it happens…" I hesitated.

"What if it happens to you," Livia finished speaking for me. I nodded, embarrassed and awkward at what I'd said. I fell silent.

Livia slipped her hand over mine. "Sometimes life doesn't go as planned, Popi. But not every woman dies in childbirth. What happens is in the lap of the gods and you cannot change their will. You must just live your life as best you can, try to keep them happy and hope that they send some luck your way," she said, and I knew in my heart that she was right. I felt better already for having spoken my fear to someone who listened and understood.

"There are some things we *can* do in life. We can sometimes help other people, if we are lucky enough to get the chance," she added.

I promised myself, there and then, I would try to remember her words always.

We stayed at Livia's for the night. Then this morning, she asked us to return in two days' time for the first day of the Festival of Diana when she says she will have another party in honour of the moon goddess, and we will all dance under the moonlight together.

27 MAY AD74

Last night, after we had all danced for Diana and after Melus had joined us, we sat out on Livia's cushions and hatched a plan between us.

"I love it out here. It's like a dream," sighed Cecilia.

"But it's not the real world. That's back in Rome, along with the noisy crowds and the crammed streets," Livia replied gently. That was my cue to say what I had been thinking in the lamplight.

"We must go back and find Longus," I blurted out. "We can talk to him, try to find out what he wants. Nobody has been listening to him. That's the problem."

"But Father wants us to stay on the farm," Cecilia said doubtfully.

Livia dived in. "Goodness, girls! With my

apologies to you, Melus, men can be led like
bulls by the nose if women can be bothered to do
it! Here we are, celebrating the goddess Diana
for her strong spirit... Did she rely on men? Of
course not! She did things for herself. Follow
her example!"

Melus looked alarmed, but stayed quiet as
Livia continued: "I'll tell you what. The Festival
of Vestalia is coming. You can say that as women
of Rome you cannot possibly miss such an
important celebration, that it would be inviting
terrible bad luck for the wedding and your
future happiness to do so. Say that you must
return to the city to visit the Temple of Vesta and
ask the goddess for her blessing. Insist!"

Cecilia looked at me, then at a nervous Melus.
She had a purposeful look on her face.

"Yes, we shall go back!" she said defiantly.

"But surely..." Melus began. Livia bent over
and tweaked his nose to shut him up.

5 JUNE AD74
THE NONES OF JUNE

When Father came home this evening we were sitting nervously waiting for him, praying he would not be too angry with us for coming back from the farm without his permission. We would have been back before, but daily downpours of rain delayed our plans and Melus wouldn't let us take any chances travelling on slippery road cobbles. I think he was in two minds about the whole thing because, although we weren't disobeying Father exactly, we weren't obeying him either. Paetas was worried, too, about getting into trouble for not stopping us, but in the end we gave him no choice but to pack up and come on home with us.

When we finally arrived this afternoon we certainly surprised Mother. She had a visitor, Cornelia's mother Julia, and the pair of them were sitting eating honey cakes when we rushed in.

"Girls! However did you…" Mother cried, before Cecilia cut her off with a gabbling explanation.

"Don't be angry! We couldn't stay away a moment longer! We must do something, and we cannot miss the Festival of Vestalia. To displease the goddess of domestic happiness would be unlucky for the wedding!"

Mother looked shocked. "Your father will be furious! Where is Paetas? He was supposed to be keeping an eye on you!" she gasped.

"He was..." Cecilia faltered.

This is going wrong already, I thought, with rising panic. But then Livia was announced behind us. She had come to try to help if our parents were angry, and when we introduced her she immediately explained that she and her slaves had escorted us home, what wonderful girls we were, how charming Dio was and how glad she was to help us all.

Julia chimed in helpfully, too. "Of course, you are absolutely right. Roman women really must go to the Temple of Vesta during the sacred festival time. We should all go, and ask the goddess to help with your family problem."

So then there were five women lined up waiting for Father when he got home. His face was a picture of surprise. He couldn't be really angry, not in public. Perhaps he might have told us off, but Livia didn't wait for him to do so. Instead she introduced herself with a very gracious speech showing how well-bred she was.

Then it was Julia's turn, who told him how sensible we had been to come home for Vestalia, and just as he was finally about to say something Mother cut in: "Isn't it wonderful to see them home? We really should give thanks to the household spirits for their safe return. I think we should do it straight away, dear. Here, take these honey cakes to the altar. I shall see our kind visitors out."

She propelled our dumbstruck Father off in the direction of our household altar, clutching the plate of cakes to lay upon it as an offering. We all agreed to visit the Temple of Vesta very soon, and by the time Father returned, Julia and Livia had left, and Mother had sent me and Cecilia to our rooms, so she could deal with him on her own. Mother can be pretty cunning. Good for her!

9 JUNE AD74

I know for sure that a divine miracle occurred today, though nobody else knows but me. I asked the goddess Vesta herself for help, and I think I got it. It began with a journey in our litter for Mother, Cecilia and me, right across the heart of Rome, through the Forum towards the Temple of Vesta. The Forum is always so exciting! It would be hard to imagine the grandness of it without seeing it – the huge space, such important buildings all around it,

THE FORUM

TEMPLE OF JUPITER – ON CAPITOL HILL

TEMPLE OF SATURN

TABULARIUM – ROMAN
STATE ARCHIVES

TEMPLE OF
CONCORDIA AUGUSTA

THE SENATE –
PARLIAMENT BUILDING

ROSTRA – SPEAKERS'
PLATFORMS

such grand statues, and so very many people.

At one point we had to stop and wait to let a fat snooty-looking senator pass, surrounded by his guards. Then we nearly bumped in to a man reading poetry out loud, and I felt quite dizzy after our bearers had to weave their way through several bunches of out-of-town tourists gawping at the statues. I'll bet one or two pickpockets stood behind them, though they'd be too fast to spot.

Eventually we came in sight of the Temple, smothered in marble and columns. What makes it really easy to spot amongst the other temples is the smoke curling up through a hole in the circular roof from the sacred fire kept burning below to please the goddess.

Livia was already inside, as were Julia and a very excited Cornelia. It was cool, and smelt so strongly of incense my eyes began to smart. There were murmurs and the rustling of ladies' long tunics as they brushed the floor. Because it was the middle of the Vestalia Festival it was a busy day, with lots of respectable ladies visiting to pay homage to the goddess and so help to ensure happiness at home. (No men, of course. They're not allowed!)

Cornelia pointed out an enclosure that she said was the room holding the Temple's sacred objects. "If only we could see them," she sighed longingly. But to do that we would have to be married and then turn up on the one day of the year they open the room.

"What are the sacred objects?" I whispered

back. "I don't know! Some kind of statues, I think. They're secret!" she replied. "Oh look!"

Suddenly a Vestal Virgin appeared in a white dress, looking very proud and tall because of her high bridal hairstyle. She moved towards the sacred fire and looked as if she was splashing liquid on the floor from a flask.

"What's she doing?" I asked Cornelia.

"She's pouring a libation, an offering to make the goddess happy. Now will be a good time to ask for her blessing," Cornelia suggested.

So I did, silently. I asked her for good fortune, and a little extra help for the Fulvius family.

I was in Livia's litter, not Mother's, when we reached home. She had asked if I would like to go with her. I agreed, and one way or another we got home first. Now I think that was all part of the miracle, I think. We hadn't even reached the door when I noticed someone watching us, lounging across the street. When he walked towards us I recognised him as one of the men I had met at the racing stables when I went searching for Longus.

"I've word for the girl," he gestured at me. Livia's slaves barred his way, not liking the look of him, but she motioned to let him through.

"Your brother, the one that was lost… you asked for information," he muttered, then went silent. I stood there, puzzled, but Livia took charge and handed him some coins that started him talking again.

"He's back in town," he said, and gave Longus's address in a different part of the city. More coins were handed over and he walked away, satisfied, as the front door opened and our head slave Nicander appeared.

"Please tell the mistress of your house that I have asked Popillia to visit me at home for an hour or so. I want to show her a new manuscript I have bought. I shall return her in good time for dinner," Livia told Nicander, and before he could reply she ordered her slaves to carry us away. I was confused, then delighted when she stopped us around the corner and gave Longus's address to her litter bearers.

"Let's catch this brother of yours and find out what's what," she grinned at me. We were off!

VIII

10 JUNE AD74

I have a big, big secret and I'm going to write it
down. It'll be like telling someone, a best friend,
and I want to do that badly, but I can't. Once
I've written it I'll have to keep the scroll hidden,
though, that's for sure. Even from Paetas.

Livia began it. After she had told Nicander
I was going to visit her for an hour or two, we
went to the address we had been given for
Longus. It was in a maze of alleyways lined
with tall buildings so rickety they looked as if
they would topple over, if they weren't jammed
so tightly together. We passed a burnt-out
building that stood out like a rotten black tooth.
Then we turned into a road where barefoot
children were playing around a water fountain,
along with a mangy dog or two. They sang and
cried out to us until someone from a balcony
above screamed at them to shut up. We stopped
by a building stretching several storeys high.

At street level, there was a crumbling boarded-up shop and I thought I saw a rat in the shadows, though I could have imagined it. I certainly couldn't imagine Longus living there.

Livia ordered her strongest-looking slave to go up inside the building. He climbed dubiously up some creaky wooden stairs and disappeared for a while. At last he came down, followed by my wary-looking stepbrother.

Livia pulled back the litter curtain and spoke to him first. "Lucius Fulvius Longus, I believe? I am Primia Decia Livia, a friend of your sister, Popillia." She pulled the curtain further back to reveal me.

"Popi!" Longus cried and I was relieved to find he was delighted to see me. "However did you find me? You won't tell Father, will you? You'd better come up. It's not grand up there but it's clean. Livia, may I offer you my hospitality?" So off up the stairs we went.

I knew by now how curious Livia was, and I certainly was, but even so, Longus's apartment building was a real eye-opener. We saw rooms leading off the stairs on different floors. Some were only screened off from the stairwell by flimsy curtains instead of doors. From the sounds we heard, the whole building seemed pretty full – adults screeching at children and each other, babies bawling, birds singing in cages… How did they all fit in?

Longus had one room but it had a balcony, and at least the window had some shutters on it

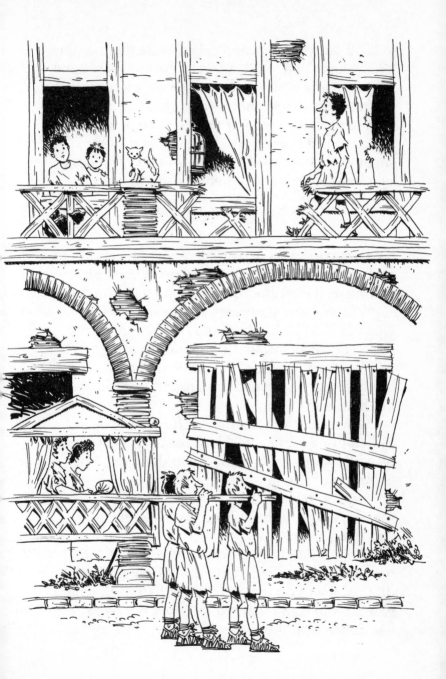

to keep out draughts and rain. Inside the room he
had a single bed (well, a pile of cushions on some
bricks), a low table, and a bucket of water carried
up from the street. There was a small heating
brazier in the corner, but no fire to cook on, so
Longus must have been living off food from
street stalls (he was definitely thinner). He looked
as if he was wearing someone else's old tunic.

"It's not bad up here, is it? I've just moved in but
everyone seems friendly," Longus remarked,
talking as if everything was completely normal.

"Where have you been, Longus? We are all
worried sick!" I cried. Longus looked guilty.
Livia stayed silent, watching and listening.

"I've been on tour," he replied. Then,
brightening, he rummaged around in a knapsack
on the floor.

"I bought you something," he said, and
pulled out a bronze necklace made in the form
of shell-shapes. "It's from down the coast," he
explained. "I've got one for Cecilia, too."

"So you meant to come home, then?" I
replied, and I couldn't keep my voice from
sounding critical.

"Popi, I had to get away! Father and I… He
was driving me crazy with his nagging. 'Don't
do this. Don't do that.' He never listens to what I
want. I told him I wanted to travel but he said I
had to start thinking about getting some awful

government job, or he might consider cutting off my allowances!" he cried. "I left and went on a tour with some of the theatre performers. It was fantastic, Popi! We did some dancing and music at a few country villas. They let me go along and bang a drum."

"Did you go on tour with Scipia, the rope-dancer?" I asked. Longus started at the sound of her name.

"No, she had a booking somewhere else," he hesitated. Livia rearranged her feet but stayed silent.

"Will you see her again?" I asked. "Father thinks…"

"Father thinks lots of things! I will see her if I wish!" he cried, then softened. "I wish you could meet her, Popi. She's amazing!"

"Will you come home and speak to Father?" I asked.

"Not if he's going to order me around," Longus replied, his lips tightening in a way that I knew meant stubbornness. The only other person I've seen do that is Father.

"Please come home, Longus! Please!" I pleaded. "Cecilia's marriage to Melus is threatened by all this." Longus looked stricken, as if he hadn't thought of this before. I wanted to scream at him for being so selfish!

"Look, I'll think about it. But don't tell Father where I am. Not yet," Longus urged, squeezing my hand.

Livia stood up. "We must leave, my dear. Time is short," she said, putting a hand lightly on my shoulder. Then she smiled graciously at Longus, who had stood up and seemed a little startled at the way she fixed him with her big brown eyes.

"Of course, of course," he said quickly. "Thank you for accompanying my sister. It was most thoughtful." I was proud of his manners. He kissed me on the cheek and told me not to worry. Then he watched us out into the litter.

"Your brother has spirit; he's impetuous, and extremely proud," Livia mused. "He hasn't married the dancer yet, though."

She seemed to think for a minute, then turned

to me. "Popi, when you get home don't tell anyone what's happened. If you do, my plan won't work."

"What plan?" I asked, confused.

"I shall ask your mother if you can visit me tomorrow for the afternoon. We shall go to the theatre."

"Oh no! I would never be allowed to do that. My father and mother don't think the theatre is respectable," I gasped.

"Well, then, we shan't tell them our plans, and I shall find you a disguise. Don't you want to meet Scipia, the lovely rope-dancer?" Livia replied, grinning mischievously at me. It's true, I do. I think she is the key to all this trouble. So, this very afternoon of the day I am writing my diary, I am going to seriously disobey my parents and go to the theatre. But before I do I must hide this scroll, so full of secrets. Gods protect it, and me!

IX

11 JUNE AD74

The actor-clowns were the best thing in the play today. They were very, very rude but I couldn't help laughing, so I was glad we were high up in the back of the theatre seats, where the women sit. I needn't have worried. The most respectable-looking ladies laughed just as much as all the men in front. I was surprised how noisy the audience were, especially at the very front where a selection of low-life was milling around.

I forget what the play was about exactly, except it involved mistaken identity, long-lost twins and a shipwreck. I reckon I could write a better one. I might try, and show it to Paetas. The actors wore Greek-style clothes, some with masks, and they spoke very loudly or sang, and waved their arms around a lot to emphasise their words. Livia explained some of the details to me: "That actor there is supposed to be a slave. They always wear red wigs. Black wigs are for young men, and grey for old ones."

"You've been to the theatre before, then?"

I remarked.

"Yes, it's fun, don't you think?" she replied. I wondered whether she had done it when she was married. If so I can't imagine her old-fashioned husband being pleased.

It was hot, even in the fresh air. A lady next to us fell asleep and snored. My 'disguise', as Livia called it, made me clammy. I had on more make-up than I've ever worn before, a wig and a dowdy tunic so nobody would look at me. But I didn't give much for my chances of avoiding being recognised if anyone I knew turned up.

After a while there was an interval in the play and some nut-sellers walked around selling their wares. There was some interval entertainment too. A flute player came on, and a cheer went up. Then Livia poked me in the ribs. "Here comes Scipia," she said, but she didn't need to point her out.

The lady coming on stage was very exotic-looking, with long black hair braided into ropes and dramatic painted eyes. Her clothes... well, there weren't all that many of them, only just enough to cover her private parts up. She swayed with a rope until you could have sworn it was a snake, and as the music got faster the crowd cheered louder.

I glanced worriedly at Livia, very shocked, but she was giggling and looking delighted. It crossed my mind that my new friend was even more mischievous than I had thought.

Scipia disappeared for the second half of the play and by the sound of it most of the audience were sorry. Of course, there weren't any women in the play and the actors dressed in female clothes just didn't have the rope-dancer's curves.

"Do you want to see the rest or shall we go and find Scipia?" Livia suggested. I nervously agreed to the latter. We collected Livia's slaves and went around to the back of the grass mound behind the stage. There was a sort of higgledy-piggledy encampment, some wooden dressing-rooms and various tents. It smelt of outdoor cooking and squashed grass. The flute player was sitting on the ground cleaning his flute. He stood up when we approached.

"The actors are still working," he grunted, and I went red. He must have thought we were obsessed fans!

"We wish to speak to Scipia," Livia explained in her best well-bred voice. At that he looked at us even more suspiciously, then nodded his head and strode off to a corner tent. When he came out Scipia was behind him.

"Ladies to see you," he remarked gruffly and went back to his flute-cleaning.

Scipia looked at us with a questioning gaze. Close up she was still stunning, with almond-shaped eyes, heavy lips and the kind of cheekbones sculptors of statues love to copy.

"I am Livia. This is my charge, Popillia. She wishes to speak with you," Livia announced, and to my surprise shoved me in the back towards Scipia's tent. "I shall leave two slaves here with you, Popillia, while I go back to see the play." She smiled at Scipia, while muttering in my ear, "Tell her everything. She's all right."

"How do you know that?" I demanded under my breath.

"I've made it my business to find out. I got my slaves to do some asking around. Trust me, Popi. This is the best way," Livia whispered. "See you later," she said to me out loud and glided graciously off, leaving her two biggest slaves behind to guard me.

Scipia looked at me kindly enough. With a, "Come on in, then," she motioned me towards the tent. What was inside really surprised me. Silken cushions were piled on the floor on top of costly rugs. Sweets sat in tiny silver bowls on a gold-painted table, and a heady rosewater scent filled the tent. On another side table there were pots of make-up and ointments, tweezers, painting sticks and so on, as well as a jewellery box and a fine mirror made of polished metal.

Scipia stared at me, then put her hand out and pulled gently at my wig.

"Please don't! It's all pinned on!" I cried.

"You have on more make-up than you are used to," she commented. "You don't look relaxed. How old are you?" I told her and she smiled. "Let's see…" She casually overturned her jewellery box and beautiful pieces spilled out on to the table. She ran her fingers over them before picking up a pair of long earrings inlaid with brown-gold stones. "Try them," she said. "They will suit your eyes."

"I couldn't… " I hesitated.

"Go on. Between you and me, I get given stuff like this all the time. Fans, you know. Some of them are richer than is good for them."

"Oh," I gasped, hoping she didn't mean my brother. I held the earrings up. Reflected in the mirror they did look fabulous.

"There. I was right," Scipia purred. She smiled with satisfaction and draped herself on her cushions. "So, a well-born young girl turns up in disguise to see a rope-dancer. What's this all about then?"

Now I was in front of Scipia I didn't know quite what to do, but I remembered what Livia had just said: "Tell her everything."

So I tentatively began to explain about Longus rowing with Father and Cecilia's wedding being put in jeopardy. My confidence was sinking, though. I had come with some vague idea that I could perhaps find a way to persuade Scipia not to marry Longus, for Cecilia's sake. But then it occurred to me that Scipia probably knew Longus's side of the story already, and she might already be upset about his family's attitude, angry even. After all, if she loved Longus she wouldn't take kindly to any idea of giving him up. And now I'd seen her performing at the theatre... Well, she'd have to change beyond all recognition if Melus's family were ever to approve the connection. There seemed no way out.

I came to the end of my explanation sure that Cecilia's wedding plans were looking hopeless, and that Father would just have to get used to Scipia the freedwoman as a daughter-in-law, and make the best of it. Scipia would have to come and live at our house, and wear a few more clothes, and... My mind was racing and for a minute I didn't notice Scipia giggling at me.

"Your brother, what was his name again?" she asked.

"Longus," I replied, astonished.

"What does he look like?" she continued. "Er, well, tall and thin, with curly hair... " I muttered.

"Hair like a mop? I know him. Merchant's son who fancies himself as a bit of a musician. Didn't he just do a tour down the coast?" Scipia asked.

"Yes. Um, he says he's going to marry you," I replied, deeply confused.

"Oh, does he?" she snorted. "Well, he's not bad-looking, if I'm thinking of the right man."

"He's in love with you!" I cried, becoming indignant on my stepbrother's behalf. Scipia smiled and offered me a plate of sticky sweets.

"When Cupid's arrow strikes, love falls where it falls. It can't be helped. Your father is a fool to deny it," she replied. "But Popillia, there are many different kinds of love in the world. Remember that. Your brother, for instance; you could call him lovestruck. He loves the *idea* of me, and imagines us together. I have got lots of young admirers like that. Often as not they are rebelling against their parents and I don't mind encouraging some of the rich ones, I admit. I'm only a freedwoman, you know. I can always do with some gifts."

"You mean you aren't going to marry Longus?" I asked wonderingly.

"That's right. He's sweet, but he's not the one for me. I can put him straight, if you like. Is that what you want, little Popi? I don't mind telling you, though; I hate all this snobbery. I don't see why a freedwoman can't marry anyone she wants."

I didn't know what to say or think, but Scipia was very kind. She pressed me to try more sweet delicacies from her silver plates. "They're from Libya, like me. That's probably another reason why your father wasn't keen on me. Romans don't mind taking charge of half the world, but a foreigner in the family? Shocking! He'd sooner walk through the Forum with no toga on, I should think!"

The sweets were soft and melting. They left a sweet, sticky taste on my lips, a mysterious taste I didn't recognise. They were strangely flavoured, different, like Scipia herself.

"Do you visit Libya?" I asked. "Sometimes, on tour," she replied, and she began to tell me some of her story. She enthralled me with her description of Libya's grand trading cities overlooking the sea, filled with rich markets selling goods from all over the world. She described the grand feasts held in the moonlight in the desert, at which she first learnt to dance for an audience when she was very young. She was born into slavery, but when her owner, also her trainer, finally died he freed her in his will.

She was a great storyteller, but when I asked if she ever wrote her stories down she shook her head.

"I never had any learning. Everyday stories like mine don't get written down," she said. "Still, I've done what I can with what the gods gave me," she winked. She was a realist, Scipia, and clever, too. I liked her very much. She would have made a very interesting sister-in-law, but she would never have put up with Longus's dreaming ways for long!

We heard activity outside the tent, which signalled the end of the play. "Go home to your happy, loving family," Scipia said. "And don't worry. I won't be rope-dancing in your garden any time soon. Here…" She pressed the earrings into my hand. "Remember what I said, Popillia. It's all very well having rules about who marries whom, but there are many different kinds of love and those who deny it are fools." She kissed me on the forehead and pulled back the tent to let me out.

I took off my make-up and wig at Livia's house and when I got home I said nothing about my secret trip. But I'm still thinking about what Scipia said. She gave me a lot to think about and I'm glad at least a tiny part of her story is now written down in my scrolls.

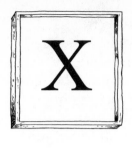

16 JUNE AD74

"Lucky day!" Paulina trilled this morning when she came to clean my room. She meant that it is officially a day of good fortune; that for weeks nobody has got married in case of bad luck, but now it's safe to do so once more. Of course, neither of us realised just how lucky the day would be for the Fulvius family!

Nicander announced the miracle to my father at lunch. "Longus is home, Sir."

I had been hoping and praying to the gods for it, especially since Atia had told me quietly what all the slaves knew, that Longus has arranged to meet Father, and that Father had seen and spoken to him – just a day or two after I went to the theatre, apparently. They must have made peace, and now there's no hiding everyone's relief! Dio ran and jumped on Longus as soon as he appeared, but things with Cecilia were a bit more touch-and-go. She ran away crying and refused to speak to him, but he went to her room and they must have made up because she soon came out dry-eyed, wearing the necklace of shell shapes he had bought her on his travels.

"I am going to pay a visit to Melus's family," Father announced. "Don't go wandering off again, Longus!" he quipped. I glanced at Longus, worried he'd take offence at that, but he simply smiled and said nothing. Father left in his smartest toga, and Mother rushed off to tell Julia the news.

Meanwhile Longus sat with us in the garden. He explained to Cecilia and Dio how he had been on tour with the musicians (I didn't show that I already knew).

"Everyone says you love a rope-dancer," Dio blurted out. At that Longus looked serious, and I stayed quiet.

"I thought I did, but it seems she does not return my feelings," Longus sighed.

"You mean she doesn't really like you?" Dio asked bluntly.

"She came to find me and made it plain that her heart belongs to another. It seems my hopes for her were a dream," Longus replied. "Apparently I will always have her good wishes but she's in love with a flute player," he added, obviously disgusted at the news. Good old Scipia. She had let him down as lightly as she could.

"And Father? Are you two reconciled?" I asked.

Longus nodded. "He has agreed to try to be more reasonable with me from day to day, and in return I have agreed to do the same. And I apologise for worrying everyone so much. I can't say I'm 'over' Scipia but I know that time will heal. I find it helps to write poetry," he said, and pulled out a scroll that had been tucked into his belt. He read out a poem about being broken-hearted. I didn't think much of it.

When he had finished, Paetas stepped out from behind a colonnade, where he had been listening. "Well done, Longus. You write what you know. I always say that is the best way, don't I, Popillia?" He gave me a funny look and I realised that he knew something! As soon as I could I got him on his own.

"You left behind your wax tablet after your lesson this morning," he said, and handed it to me. I'd used the tablet to scratch a few notes on the play, ready to try writing my own version later on. The notes still showed up on the wax.

"Looking at these jottings, I would say the person who wrote them had definitely made a personal visit to the theatre recently," he remarked, and handed me the tablet. "I'd wipe that clean if I were you. You might well need it for tomorrow."

"Why?" I asked.

"There is to be a ceremony, I believe. Cecilia and Melus will become officially engaged. You might want to make notes," he replied, with an amused look on his face. How come Paetas always knows everything?

18 June AD74

Yesterday, when Melus gave Cecilia an iron ring, my eyes just filled up, so I was looking through a blur as he put it on her ring finger and bound the nerve leading from there to her heart. I'm not ashamed to admit I cried. I was beginning to think they'd never get this far. Now they've made their engagement vows and the stage is all set for their coming wedding.

The biggest surprise of all was that I actually wished it was my turn. Perhaps I've done some growing up without even noticing. I've certainly had a very eventful time, and I think that's taken my mind off worrying about life. I think Livia is right. There are some things I can't change in my life. They are the choice of the gods and there's no point fretting over them. But there are some things I can alter, and I've proved it by making sure this wedding goes ahead!

The very best food was on offer for the engagement dinner. Melus's parents seemed pleasant enough, which was a relief, as Cecilia will be going to live with them. So now it's just a question of getting ready for the big event. Paetas has been asked to write the invitations in his neatest hand. He has started today, and I saw there was one for Livia. This wedding could be even more fun than I thought!

XI

22 JUNE AD74

Yesterday, the night before her wedding, Cecilia laid her childhood toys on the household altar, along with the lucky locket that I've seen her wear for as long as I can remember. When I saw her do that, I touched my own locket. It has warded off evil since I was born. I silently thanked the gods for Cecilia's happiness, and for showing me that growing up needn't be scary. It can be fun too!

This morning Mother tied a wedding belt around Cecilia's pure white dress, and tied it in two big knots that only Melus would be allowed to touch. Cecilia looked like some magical figure from a wall painting as she stood under the flower garlands and tree boughs decorating our house for the wedding day. We draped the flame-coloured veil over her specially styled hair, and she slipped her feet into matching red wedding shoes. I placed on her head the circlet of flowers she had made herself.

"You look like a statue, Ceci!" Dio cried. He

was all scrubbed and brushed to look smart, and at last, Longus was there, too, wearing a new toga and looking the part of the handsome young master of the house. Nicander announced the arrival of Melus, who strode in looking as happy as Cecilia looked beautiful. Now the ceremonies could begin in the atrium.

Cornelia's father, being a suitable family friend, acted as priest. He sacrificed a small pig, slit open its stomach and peered at its liver to read the omens for the day. "Perfect," he announced. "Everything points towards good luck."

"What if the omens were bad?" Dio whispered to me. "They never look bad on wedding days," Longus told him quietly. "At least, no one ever admits it," he chuckled.

Meanwhile the slaves were kept busy opening the door to all the smartly dressed guests. Livia arrived, and I panicked for a moment when Mother introduced her to Longus, thinking they had never met and never guessing that Livia and I had visited him in his secret flat! I needn't have worried, though, because, of course, they didn't let her know, though they smiled knowingly at each other once she had walked away.

Everyone gathered in the atrium ready for the marriage. Julia, being an upstanding married woman, was acting as matron-of-honour.

She took Cecilia's hand and gave her to Melus, and I felt thrilled for them.

"I'm hungry!" Dio said.

"Sshh, this is the important bit!" Longus muttered in his ear.

Melus made his vow. "Where I am Decius, you are Decia," he said, conferring his family name on Cecilia.

"Where you are Decius, I am Decia," Cecilia replied, accepting it.

There were cheers and cries of 'Good luck to you!' from the guests as the witnesses put their seals on the marriage contract.

"Are they married now?" Dio asked.

"Yes. You're in luck, Dio. It's time for the wedding meal. Last to the table is a squashed cockroach!" Longus laughed.

There were lots of plates of dainties and things on sticks, plus flasks of good wine, and we all tucked in happily. Then, halfway through, a really odd thing happened. Nicander handed me a small plate of unusual gold-coloured sweets.

"What are these?" I asked.

"They were left at the house as a wedding gift," he said to me. "Whoever delivered them asked especially that they be offered to you first." I nibbled one, and recognised the distinctive taste of spicy sweetness I had last experienced in Scipia's tent.

"They look unusual," Livia commented, looking over my shoulder and picking up a sweet. "Mmm, very exotic." The noise of the crowd grew louder and jollier as the married pair were given gifts, mostly money.

"Are you enjoying yourself, Popi?" Longus asked. He seemed to be turning up wherever Livia went.

"Oh yes! Of course," I replied.

"Weddings are all right, I suppose... generally," he remarked.

"When people are really fond of each other," Livia added. It struck me that this kind of day might be hard for her, after her own divorce. But she is still very young and she could marry again, quite easily. She is rich and fun; someone will fall for her... But she is prone to being impetuous just like Longus, and doesn't mind doing things that will shock people – marrying a younger man of lower rank, possibly? Oh, Jupiter! What have I done, introducing those two?

"Procession time!" Father announced and the guests made space for Cecilia, Mother and Melus. Cecilia pretended to clutch Mother's arm and Melus pulled her away, with a comical, stern look on his face, as everyone laughed and cheered around them.

"What's going on? Doesn't Cecilia want to go?" Dio asked anxiously.

"It's all right; they're only play acting. It's traditional," Longus explained. "Are you all set, Dio? It's time for you to do your job. You're very important, you know!"

With a serious look of concentration on his face Dio lined up with two other boys, ready to escort Cecilia to Melus's house. Father handed him a wooden torch lit from the family hearth. "Off you go, boys," Father cried and we all moved out of the house as the boys led Cecilia into the street. Nuts clattered on to the path, thrown by guests.

"May the bride be fertile," someone cried and we all set out behind the couple, laughing, joking and singing.

"See you later," Livia waved to us, as the groom's family split off from the bride's crowd to get to Melus's house before us. Then our procession began to sing the traditional (and very rude) wedding songs as we marched along.

"Isn't this fun? I think I might do it myself soon," Longus said, squeezing my elbow. I must have looked worried because he laughed out loud. "Just teasing!" he said. "I want to see the world before I settle down. Father and I have agreed that I am not going to try to claw my way into the Senate, but I am going to work for him instead. I'll be travelling abroad regularly."

"Oh Longus, that's great news. You are lucky, I'd love to travel, too," I replied.

"Then you must marry someone who will take you. Roman ladies can't simply go off on their own where they please," he grinned. I chuckled to myself, thinking he still had some things to learn about our new friend, Livia. Do you know, it might not be such a bad thing if they did get together. They could go travelling and take me with them...

By now we had reached the front door of Melus's home. Cecilia anointed the doorway with oil, and handed over to him a weaving spindle and a household staff, to show what a good housewife she was going to be. Then Melus came out and lifted Cecilia up over the front step, so she wouldn't trip and bring bad luck into the household. It was a moment I'll always remember.

After that we all piled into the house and the fun went on until it was time for Father to hand Cecilia over to Melus once more, and they were led off to their marriage bed. It was decorated with branches and flowers. By the time we got home it was late evening, but I've stayed up to write by lamplight, while it's all fresh in my mind. Tomorrow Cecilia will wake up a married woman, a matron of senatorial rank, much to Father's delight. Dio will probably sleep in after all the wine and excitement. And me? Hmm, all I need to do is get Livia and Longus together… And then get Father and Mother to agree to let me go travelling with them… But first I'll need to go out and get some more scrolls. I've run out, and I've got the rest of my life to write about – and that's going to be even more exciting than the last few weeks have been!

FACT FILE

ROMAN WOMEN

Roman women had fewer rights than men. First of all, they were under the control of their fathers, then after marriage, their husbands. However, when they married they kept control of their own wealth, which helped them to be more independent. Also, it was relatively easy to divorce. If a woman divorced her husband she then went back to her father's home. If her father was already dead, she would be fully independent, but was expected to marry again. Many women died in childbirth, so men often married more than once.

ROMAN LEARNING

Until the age of seven, boys and girls were taught at home by their mother or by a tutor, usually a slave. At the age of seven boys went to a school, but girls stopped their education and were taught home skills instead.

COMING OF AGE

Normally, boys wore a crimson-edged toga. When their father decided they had come of age, at about the age of fourteen, there was a special ceremony. The boy changed into a pure white toga and there was a procession to the Forum to add his name to the list of Roman citizens.

DRESS FOR WOMEN

Girls wore a simple short tunic belted around the middle. Women wore long tunics, but once they were married they wore another long sleeveless garment over the top, called a 'stola'.

TUNIC

PLEASING THE GODS

STOLA

There were lots of religious festivals through the year in Rome, and that made arranging a wedding date complicated. Religious festival days had to be avoided, and also any unlucky days, such as the Ides of the month. Romans were extremely superstitious. At ceremonies, such as weddings, they made animal sacrifices to try to please their gods and goddesses.

GLOSSARY

Here are some explanations of Roman words from Popillia's story.

BATHHOUSE

Romans liked to bathe every day. Rich family villas had their own private bathhouses, with underfloor heating and plumbing. In Rome, there were lots of public baths too.

COLONNADE

A row of pillars. Roman villas often had colonnades around an internal garden.

EMPEROR

The all-powerful leader of the Roman Empire.

FORUM

The main centre of Rome, a big public square decorated with statues and lined with important buildings.

LITTER

A kind of chair carried around by slaves, with curtains around it for privacy.

SCROLL

A sheet of paper made from papyrus reed. For storage it was attached to a round piece of wood at either end, so it could be rolled and unrolled. Romans wrote on scrolls with ink.

SENATORS

Males who belonged to the Senate, part of Rome's government. Men had to own a certain amount of land and money to qualify as a senator. Many of them were from noble Roman families.

SLAVES

People who were the property of their owners. They could be bought and sold.

TABLET

A small wooden board with raised edges, filled with wax. Romans wrote notes on the wax using a stylus, a stick made from bone or metal. The stylus was pointed at one end to make marks, and flat at the other end so that the marks could be wiped away.

VILLA

A one-storey Roman house. The richer the Roman, the larger and more splendid the villa he or she owned. Many families had country villas too, set on farm estates outside Rome.

OTHER TITLES IN THIS SERIES

THE DIARY OF A YOUNG ROMAN SOLDIER
Marcus Gallo travels to Britain with his legion to help pacify the wild Celtic tribes.

THE DIARY OF A YOUNG TUDOR LADY-IN WAITING
Young Rebecca Swann joins her aunt as a lady-in-waiting to Queen Elizabeth the First.

THE DIARY OF A YOUNG NURSE IN WORLD WAR II
Jean Harris is hired to train as a nurse in a London hospital just as World War II breaks out.

THE DIARY OF A YOUNG WEST INDIAN IMMIGRANT
It is 1961 and Gloria Charles travels from Dominica to Britain to start a new life.

THE DIARY OF A 1960s TEENAGER
Teenager Jane Leachman is offered a job working in swinging London's fashion industry.

THE DIARY OF A YOUNG MEDIEVAL SQUIRE
It is 1332 and young William De Combe travels with his uncle to a faraway jousting competition.

THE DIARY OF SAMUEL PEPYS'S CLERK
It is 1665 and young Roger Scratch travels to London to work for his kinsman Pepys.

THE DIARY OF A WORLD WAR II PILOT
It is 1938 and young Johnny Hedley joins up to become a pilot in Britain's Royal Air Force.